Byron the Bear and the BULLY

written and illustrated by naif j. faris

This book is for those who have ever been laughed at, made fun of, or told that they were anything less than they are. A bully is someone who finds pleasure in making others feel bad. Make yourself feel good...don't listen. Keep those shoulders back, chin up, smile wide. For today will bring happiness, if you allow it.

Thank you for all those who believed in me. And for those who once bullied me, I appreciate you too. You have showed me that walking away can lead to better things. Thank you to my mother who loved and supported me through my toughest times. Growing up isn't easy for anyone. Love your flaws, embrace them, and never let anyone tell you that your weaknesses have no value. Every ounce of who you are is worth something.

naif j. faris

Byron woke up super early. He wanted to get to school in a hurry.

Today is the first day of Class! Byron had waited all Summer for break to pass.

"Welcome to the first day of school. I am your teacher, Ms. McCool."

ATTENDANCE CHART

Ben							
Breanna							
Byron							
Bryce							
Brynn							
Chris							
Don							
George							
Jo							
John							
Mike							
Norman							
Rita							
Rob							
Sam							
Sonia							
Stewy							

Byron looked around the class to make new friends. There was, Rob, Jo, Breanna, and Ben.

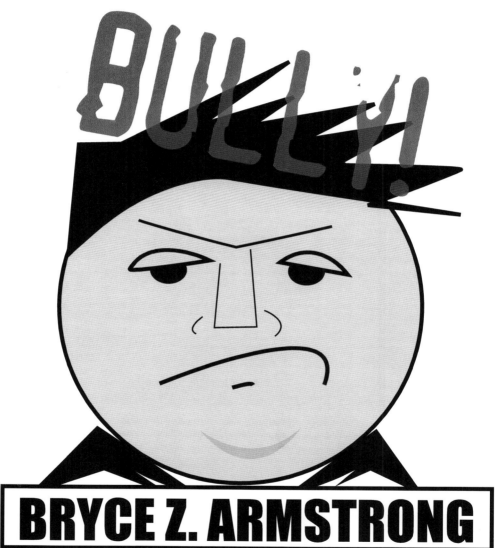

Everybody in Ms. McCool's class
seemed nice, everybody except the
school bully named Bryce.

Byron was now a little scared. Bryce was intimidating with his stare.

Byron didn't know what to do so he looked away. He couldn't wait until recess so he could play.

Ms. McCool closed her book and said, "we are done, let's go to recess and have some fun!"

Byron was excited and started to giggle. And then he felt a tickle.

It was Bryce the Bully who stood behind him. "I don't like you Bear", he said with a grin. "Until you leave I'm going to pick on you. I'll laugh and make fun of all that you do."

Byron spoke softly as his voice began to shake..."please don't beat me up for goodness sake!"

Byron closed his eyes and waited for a punch.

Without looking back Byron ran fast. To the principal's office he was at last.

His name is Bryce and he's 30 feet tall.
Standing next to him I am rather small.

Byron sat down and listened fully. He would soon be ready to confront his bully.

It was now lunch time and Bryce was waiting for the Bear. Byron walked up slowly saying a silent prayer.

Bryce approached Byron and he said..."where's my lunch? Or do you want this pie on your head?!"

Byron took a deep breath and remembered what he was taught. He took a step back and said, "Bryce this must stop!"

I am different than you and the rest of the school.
That is ok, being unique is what makes us cool.

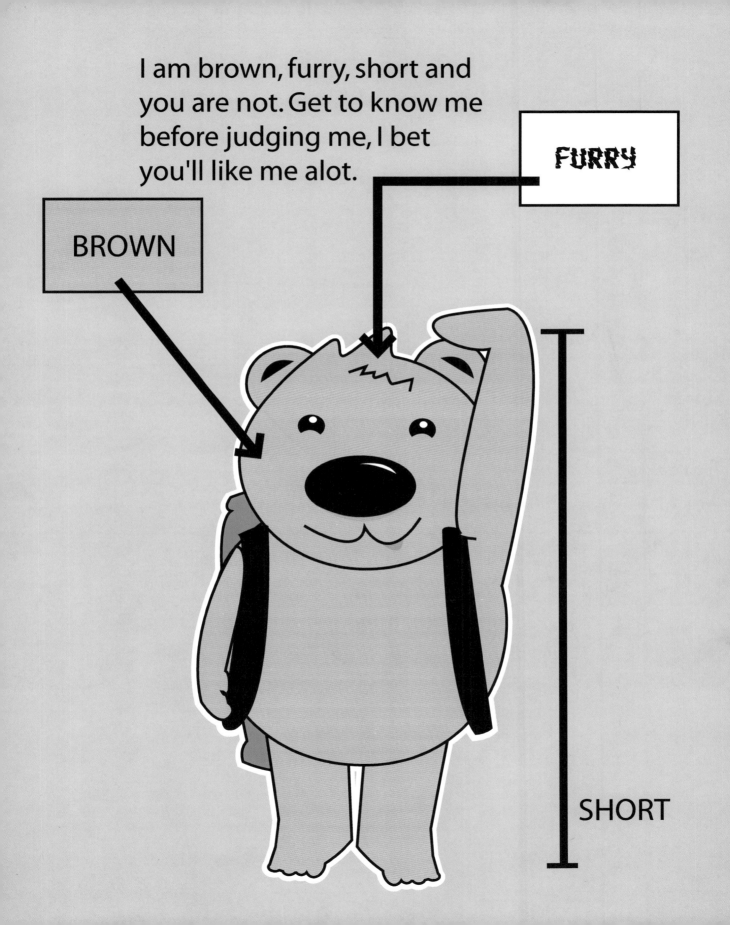

There is no reason to pick on kids for who they are.
Being mean to others wont get you very far.

Does picking on others make you feel good inside? Does making fun of me give you a sense of pride?

Let's talk about our differences, let's not fight. Put down your fists, let's make things right.

I don't want to wear the pie, I'd rather eat a slice. Stop the name calling? Try to be nice?

So shake my hand? We can start fresh from here. My name is Byron, Byron the Bear.

Byron, I appreciate your help in changing my ways. I will be kind to others for the rest of my days.

If you are being bullied let someone know. They can help you out, they can take control.

Made in the USA